"Of course," said Billy Mink, "you and I are safe enough." FRONTISPIECE. *See page 24.*

Billy Mink

THORNTON W. BURGESS

Illustrated by Harrison Cady

PUBLISHED IN ASSOCIATION WITH THE
THORNTON W. BURGESS SOCIETY,
SANDWICH, MASSACHUSETTS
BY
DOVER PUBLICATIONS, INC.
MINEOLA, NEW YORK

DOVER CHILDREN'S THRIFT CLASSICS

EDITOR OF THIS VOLUME: JANET BAINE KOPITO

Copyright

Copyright © 2012 by Dover Publications, Inc.
All rights reserved.

Bibliographical Note

This Dover edition, first published by Dover Publications, Inc., in 2012 in association with the Thornton Burgess Society, Sandwich, Massachusetts, who have provided a new Introduction, is an unabridged republication of the work published by Little, Brown and Company, Boston, in 1924.

Library of Congress Cataloging-in-Publication Data

Burgess, Thornton W. (Thornton Waldo), 1874–1965.
   Billy Mink / Thornton W. Burgess ; illustrated by Harrison Cady.
      p. cm.
   Summary: Follow the adventure of a mischievous mink and his forest friends.
   ISBN-13: 978-0-486-48107-4 — ISBN-10: 0-486-48107-7 (pbk.)
   1. Minks—Fiction. 2. Forest animals—Fiction. 3. Friendship—Fiction.]
I. Cady, Harrison, 1877–1970 ill. II. Title.

PZ7.B917Bd 2012
[Fic]—dc23

2011044485

Manufactured in the United States by Courier Corporation
48107702
www.doverpublications.com

Introduction to the Dover Edition

The keen-witted Billy Mink first appeared in Thornton Burgess's syndicated "Bedtime Stories" in newspapers in 1919. After five years of "guest appearances," he finally got his own book, originally published by Little, Brown, and Company in 1924, a big year in the author's life.

That year, Burgess bought the beautiful property in Hampden, Massachusetts, which he named "Laughing Brook," a place that became the heart of his writing life. It was also the year he launched his own radio show, "The Radio Nature League," on WBZ, then in East Springfield. Its purpose was the same as that of his books: to entertain and educate people about nature. His only pay for doing that half-hour weekly show was a ride to and from the studio, but he continued it for ten years because he believed in it. Burgess even cancelled a sponsor for interfering too much in the show.

Billy Mink, of course, has lasted much longer than the "Radio Nature League," having been reprinted several times prior to Dover's republication in 2012. Billy's book was the first of *The Smiling Pool Series*. Along with "Billy Mink," the series included *Little Joe*

Otter, Jerry Muskrat at Home, and *Longlegs the Heron.* These were the last Burgess books to be devoted to a single dominant character with a continuous narrative. After *Longlegs,* every full-length book is a collection of stories featuring different birds and animals.

Thornton Burgess says of Billy, "It is probable that few, if any, of the little people of the Green Forest and the Green Meadows are filled with fear as seldom as is Billy Mink." He is a kind of super-hero of the little folk. He is equally at home on land or in the water, and no other animal combines his abilities to swim, track, hunt, climb, think, and fight. He never loses. In this book he outwits Man, eludes predators bigger than he is, and defeats an entire colony of rats. We should all be so gifted. Turn the page and let the fun begin.

JOHN RICHMOND
The Thornton W. Burgess Society
Sandwich, Massachusetts

Contents

Illustrations

Chapter I

Billy Mink Becomes Suspicious

The stranger and the unknown must
Be always looked on with distrust.
Billy Mink.

OF all the little people in the Green Forest there is none with sharper eyes and keener wits than Billy Mink. Nothing goes on along the Laughing Brook, from where it starts in the Green Forest to where it joins the Big River, that Billy Mink doesn't know about. Billy is a great traveler. He is so full of life and energy that he cannot keep still very long at a time. Moreover, Billy is one of those little people to whom it makes no difference whether jolly, round, bright Mr. Sun is shining or gentle Mistress Moon has taken his place up in the sky, or the Black Shadows have wrapped everything in darkness. He takes a nap whenever he feels sleepy. Whenever he doesn't feel sleepy he travels back and forth up and down the Laughing Brook.

In these little journeys back and forth nothing escapes Billy's bright eyes and sharp ears and keen nose. Being such a slim fellow, he slips in and out of holes and hiding-places which no one save his cousin, Shadow the Weasel, could get into. Now it happened that one day Billy curled up in a hollow log under a pile of brush close to the Laughing Brook. In a jiffy he was asleep. Right in the very middle of the pleasantest of pleasant dreams he was awakened. Instantly he was wide awake. He was just as wide awake as if he hadn't been asleep at all. Without stopping to think anything about it, he knew what had awakened him. Some one had just passed his hiding-place.

Noiselessly Billy crept out of the hollow log and peeped from under the pile of brush. Walking down the bank of the Laughing Brook was a man.

"I've never seen that fellow before," muttered Billy to himself. "It isn't Farmer Brown's boy and it isn't Farmer Brown. He seems to be looking for something. I wonder what he is about. I think I'll watch him."

So, as silently as a shadow, Billy Mink followed the man down the Laughing Brook, and the man didn't once suspect it. You see, Billy can always find a hiding-place if it be no more than a heap of brown leaves. He just slipped from one hiding-place to another, always keeping the man in sight.

Billy became more and more interested and inquisitive as he watched that man. The man certainly did seem to be looking for something. He would examine every half-sunken log in the Laughing Brook. He searched carefully along each bank. He looked into every little hole. It didn't take Billy long to discover that this man seemed to be especially

"I've never seen that fellow before,"
muttered Billy to himself. *Page 2.*

interested in those places where Billy almost always went when traveling up and down the Laughing Brook.

Billy stopped and rubbed his nose thoughtfully. He was growing suspicious. "I wonder," thought Billy, "if he is looking for me."

Chapter II

Billy Finds a Trap

True wisdom watches closest where
There seems least cause for fear or care.
Billy Mink.

FOR two days Billy Mink saw nothing more of the man who had made him suspicious. But this didn't make Billy feel any easier in his mind. He had a feeling that the man had visited the Laughing Brook and the Smiling Pool for no good purpose. He had a feeling that his visit had something to do with himself. So Billy became more watchful than ever and traveled up and down the length of the Laughing Brook more often than ever, trying with eyes and nose to find out just what that man had been about.

On the third day the man came again. Billy saw him almost as soon as he reached the Laughing Brook, but not quite. The man had come down the Laughing Brook a little way before Billy had discovered him. Just as he had done the first time, Billy followed the man. Just as before, the man seemed to be looking for something. Billy watched him until finally he tramped off through the Green Forest. Then Billy turned and hurried back to the place where he had first seen the man that morning.

"He didn't do anything while I watched him but poke about and seem to be looking for something," muttered Billy. "I wonder if he did anything else before I discovered him. I think I'll look and make sure that everything is all right up the Laughing Brook."

So Billy went up the Laughing Brook above the place where he had first seen the man that morning. He crossed back and forth from one bank to the other, and he examined every stick and log and hole as he went along. Being suspicious, he took the greatest care not to step anywhere until he had first looked to make sure that it was safe.

His nose told him just where the man had been, but for some time he found nothing suspicious. Everything was just as it should be. Nevertheless, Billy was filled with uneasiness. He couldn't get rid of a feeling that something was wrong somewhere. Presently he came to a hole in the bank, a hole with which he was very familiar. From that hole came the most appetizing smell. Now Billy was hungry. He had spent so much time following that strange man that for some time he had had no chance to eat.

The smell from that hole was of fish. That fish was in the back of the hole. There was no doubt about that. All Billy had to do was to go in and get it, and that is what he was tempted to do. Then in a flash a thought came to him. There never had been a fish there before, so why should there be one now? With the greatest care Billy began to examine everything around that hole. In the water, just at the entrance to that hole, were some dead leaves held down by a little bit of mud. Billy didn't remember ever seeing those leaves before. Very cautiously he reached out and lifted them. Underneath was a trap!

Chapter III

Billy Outwits the Trapper

As smart and clever as you are,
A Mink may smarter be by far.
Billy Mink.

THIS is what Billy Mink said to himself as he uncovered the trap which had been set for him at the entrance to one of his favorite holes in the bank of the Laughing Brook. Of course he was thinking of the trapper when he said it. At first Billy flew into a great rage. It made him angry clear to the tip of his brown tail just to think that he must now be always watching for traps where for so long there had been no danger.

At first he had thought to go on at once up the Laughing Brook and see what more he could discover. But you remember that Billy was hungry and that there was a piece of perfectly delicious fish back in that hole. He knew now just how that fish happened to be there. He knew that the trapper had put that piece of fish in there, hoping that Billy would be so eager to get it that he would be careless.

The more he smelled it, the more he wanted it. "It will serve that trapper right if I get that fish," muttered Billy. "Perhaps it will teach him that he is not so smart as he thinks he is."

Billy sat down and studied the trap and the entrance to the hole. The more he studied, the more sure he became that he would be running a very foolish risk if he tried to step over that trap just to get a piece of fish. You see, that trap had been very cunningly placed. But the more he smelled that fish, the more he wanted it.

Billy stroked his whiskers thoughtfully. Of course that didn't have anything to do with it, but just the same while he was stroking them he remembered something. His eyes snapped and he grinned. Way up on the bank between the roots of a certain tree was a little hole. It was the entrance to a little underground tunnel, and that tunnel led right down to the very hole in front of which the trap was set. It really was a back door.

Billy turned and in a flash had scrambled up the bank. With his keen little nose he made sure that there was no scent of the trapper up there. He felt sure the trapper had not found that little hole between the roots of a certain tree. But though he was sure of this, he took no chances. As he approached the hole he took the greatest care to make sure no trap was in there.

There was none. Once inside the hole, Billy ran along that little tunnel, chuckling to himself. He knew that now there was no danger. He could get that fish. He did get it. He got it and ate it right there. Then he turned and ran out the way he had entered. Somehow that fish had tasted the best of any fish he ever had eaten. It was because he had outwitted the trapper.

Chapter IV

Billy Finds Some Queer Fences

When something new and strange you find,
Watch out! To danger be not blind.
Billy Mink.

THE trouble with a great many people is that they are heedless. When they find something new and strange they forget everything but their curiosity. Because of this they walk right straight into trouble. It happens over and over again.

But Billy Mink isn't this kind of a person. My, my, I should say not. He never has been. If he had he would have lost that beautiful, brown coat of his long ago and there would be no Billy Mink. Billy has his share of curiosity, but with it he possesses a great big bump of suspicion. When he finds anything new and strange he wants to learn all about it. But right away he is suspicious of it.

After he had discovered the trap set for him at the entrance to one of his favorite holes, and had fooled the trapper by getting the fish the trapper had placed in that hole, Billy went on up the Laughing Brook to see what else he could discover. Not very far above that place there was a steep bank on each side of the Laughing Brook. Along the foot of each bank was a narrow strip of level ground between the bank and the water. You see, at this season of the year, the water in the Laughing Brook was low.

When Billy came to this place he discovered something queer. It was a little fence. It ran from the foot of the bank straight out into the Laughing Brook to where the water became deep. Midway in this little fence was a gateway just big enough to slip through comfortably. Billy looked across to the other side of the Laughing Brook. Over there was another little fence just like this one, and that little fence had an opening in it.

"Huh!" said Billy. "Huh! These fences are something new. They were not here when I came down the Laughing Brook yesterday. I wonder what they are for. If it were not for those two little openings I would have either to climb the bank or swim around the ends of those fences, and that would be bothersome. I can go through that little opening there as easily as rolling off a log. But I'm not going to do it. No, sir, I'm not going to do it. There is something wrong about these fences. They look to me as if they were built just to make me go through one of those little gateways. If that's the case, I'm not going to do it."

So Billy plunged into the Laughing Brook and swam out into the deep water around the end of the little fence. Then very carefully he approached the little opening from that side. The more he looked at it, the less he liked it. Right in the middle of that little opening were some wet, dead leaves. "Ha, ha!" said Billy. "Another trap!"

Chapter V

A Moonlight Visit

Do a good turn for another,
Proving thus you are his brother.
Billy Mink.

BILLY Mink was just plain mad. He had begun to get that way when he found the trap set at the entrance to one of his favorite holes. But when he found a little fence on each side of the Laughing Brook right across where he was in the habit of running when traveling up and down the Laughing Brook, and in the middle of each little fence an opening with a trap in it, Billy lost his temper completely. He ground his teeth and his eyes grew red with anger. You see, he knew that those traps had been set especially for him.

"I despise a trapper," snarled Billy. "Yes, sir, I despise a trapper. It is bad enough to be hunted, but then a fellow does have some chance. He knows where the danger is and what to look out for. If he is reasonably smart he can fool the hunter. But traps don't give a fellow any chance at all. They are sneaky things. They jump up and grab a fellow without any warning at all. I hate traps, and I hate trappers! I wonder if I can find any more traps along the Laughing Brook."

14

Billy continued on up to the very beginning of the Laughing Brook, but found no more traps. Then he curled up in one of his favorite hiding-places to rest and think things over. He was strongly tempted to go away from the Laughing Brook altogether. He thought of going down to the Big River for a long visit. He felt sure that if he kept away from the Laughing Brook the trapper would become discouraged and after a while take up his traps. He had just about made up his mind to leave that very night when he happened to remember that while he knew all about those traps, he had friends who didn't know anything about them. "I guess I'll stay around awhile and see what happens," muttered Billy.

That night Billy went for another look at those traps. By and by a little noise caught his quick ears. Instantly he was alert and watchful. There was a rustling of leaves, and then out on an old log full in the moonlight crept a plump form and sat down. One glance was enough for Billy. Without a sound he slipped up behind that plump form.

"Booh!" said Billy. When he said that Bobby Coon almost fell into the Laughing Brook, he was so startled. You see it was Bobby who had come out on that old log, and at the time he was very busy washing some food. You know he always washes his food before eating, if he can.

For a minute Bobby lost his temper. But it was only for a minute. Then, having washed his food to his satisfaction, he began to eat his supper and at

Out on an old log full in the moonlight crept
a plump form and sat down. *Page 15*.

the same time to gossip with Billy Mink. He told Billy all the news of the Green Forest, most of which was no news at all to Billy, for there is little going on that Billy doesn't know. Then Billy told Bobby the news of the Laughing Brook, everything except about the traps and trapper. It was a very pleasant visit they had together there in the moonlight.

Chapter VI

Billy Warns Bobby Coon

A moment's carelessness may bring
A sudden end to everything.
                              Billy Mink.

FOR a long time Billy Mink and Bobby Coon sat gossiping on the edge of the Laughing Brook. Then Bobby, having finished what he had to eat, decided that he would go down the Laughing Brook to see what he could find. There's nothing Bobby Coon enjoys more than wandering along the Laughing Brook, watching for a little fish to come carelessly within reach, or just simply playing in the water. Bobby has almost as much curiosity as has Peter Rabbit. He simply has to examine everything which appears strange. A white pebble in the water or a shell will catch his eyes, and he will stop to play with it.

Billy Mink watched Bobby start along down the Laughing Brook. "I wonder what he'll do when he comes to that little fence," thought Billy. So, to find out what Bobby would do, he followed him. When Bobby came to the little fence he sat down and stared at it in the funniest way. Then he began to talk to himself.

"That's a funny thing," said he. "I wonder how that little fence happens to be here. I've never seen it before. I wonder what it's for. Nobody had any business to build a fence like that. The only way I can get around it is to climb way up that bank, and I don't want to do that." You know Bobby is rather lazy.

So he sat and looked at the fence, which was made of sticks stuck down in the ground, and the more he looked the more determined he became that he wouldn't be stopped and he wouldn't climb that bank. Of course it didn't take him long to discover that right in the middle of that fence was an opening, sort of a gateway. But it was a very narrow opening. You see, it had been made just wide enough for Billy Mink, and Bobby Coon is a great deal bigger than Billy Mink.

Bobby went a little nearer and once more sat down with his head cocked on one side as he studied that little opening. "It's too narrow for me, but if I try hard enough, perhaps I can push those sticks aside and make it wider. That would be easier than climbing that steep bank," thought he.

So Bobby walked a few steps nearer and again sat down. Somehow, he had an uncomfortable feeling that something was wrong. He didn't know why he had that feeling, but he had it. Now whenever one of the little people of the Green Forest has that feeling he becomes very cautious. Bobby was tempted to try at once to push his way through that little opening, but because of that feeling that something was wrong he hesitated. Then very carefully he examined that little fence, from the bottom of the steep bank clear to the edge of the water. He smelled of each separate stick of that fence but he could smell nothing suspicious. Those were just plain old sticks and nothing else. Finally he made up his mind that there couldn't be anything really wrong in at least trying to go through that little opening. He reached forward with one foot to place it right in the middle of that opening.

"Stop!" cried Billy Mink.

Chapter VII

Bobby and Billy Put Their Heads Together

Oh, if we but always knew
What to do or not to do.
Billy Mink.

WHEN Billy Mink cried "Stop!" Bobby Coon stopped. He stopped with one paw lifted and just ready to put it down in the middle of the little opening in that fence which had so puzzled him. He turned his head to look back at Billy Mink. "Why should I stop?" he demanded, and he spoke rather crossly.

"Because, if you take one more step ahead, it will be the last step you ever will take," snapped Billy.

Bobby didn't take that step. Instead he backed away in such a hurry that it really was funny. You would have thought that he had burned his toes. Then he turned to face Billy Mink. "What sort of nonsense is this?" he growled. "I don't see anything wrong."

Billy grinned. "You may not see anything wrong," said he, "but if you had put your foot down in that little opening you would have felt something wrong. Yes, indeed, you would have felt something wrong! You certainly would. There is a trap hidden there.

21

I suspect it was set for me, but I guess the trapper who set it would almost as soon catch you as me."

Bobby Coon blinked and looked very hard at Billy Mink to see if he were fooling. When he saw the angry red in Billy's eyes, he knew that Billy wasn't fooling.

"Goodness, that was a narrow escape!" exclaimed Bobby. "I'm ever so much obliged to you, Billy Mink. I hope that some day I can do something for you. If you hadn't happened along to-night, I guess I would be in a terrible fix right now. Do you suppose that trapper built that little fence?"

"Of course," retorted Billy Mink. "He built it so that the only way of going up or down the Laughing Brook without taking a lot of trouble would be to go through that little opening, and no one could get through that little opening without stepping in that trap. There's another one set just the same way on the other side of the Laughing Brook."

Bobby Coon looked across and for the first time he saw the other little fence. Bobby's face became very sober. "We ought to do something about those traps," said he. "We are the only ones who know anything about them, and we can't sit here all the time to warn others who may be traveling up and down the Laughing Brook. I wouldn't want my worst enemy to be caught in one of those dreadful traps. What can we do to warn others?"

"I don't know," replied Billy Mink. "I guess we'll have to put our heads together and think up something. You know two heads are better than one."

Bobby nodded. "Let's go back to that old log there and talk it over," said he. And this is just what they did.

Chapter VIII

What Bobby Coon and Billy Mink Did

By him who seeks is knowledge gained,
And thus may wisdom be attained.
Billy Mink.

BOBBY Coon and Billy Mink sat on an old log on the bank of the Laughing Brook and talked over the traps Billy Mink had discovered and what should be done about them.

"Of course," said Billy Mink, "you and I are safe enough. We know exactly where those traps are, and we are not going to be so foolish as to get caught in one of them. But there are others who travel up and down the Laughing Brook who might not discover the traps until too late."

Bobby Coon nodded his head. "Just what I was thinking," said he. "But for you, Billy Mink, I would be in that trap down there this very minute. It was stupid of me not to have suspected that the little opening in that fence was left purposely to tempt whoever came along to go through it, instead of taking the trouble to climb that steep bank and go around the fence. There may be others just as stupid. We ought to do something about it, but what can we do?"

"Are you afraid to go near that trap?" demanded Billy.

Bobby scratched his head thoughtfully. "How near?" he asked.

"Near enough to get your paw under it," replied Billy.

"I don't know," replied Bobby. "What good will that do?"

"Well, you see," replied Billy, "that trap is set right in the middle of that little opening, and it has been covered with wet, dead leaves. Now I know something about traps. I've seen a lot of them in my day. If any one should step on those wet leaves, two steel jaws would snap up and grab him by the leg. But those steel jaws always snap *up*. They can't snap the other way. If your paw is *underneath* the trap, there is no danger. By doing this you can lift that trap up so that it will no longer be covered with those dead leaves, and whoever comes along will see it. It isn't safe to try to pull the leaves off of it, because you might get caught doing it. If you will do that to the trap on this side, I will do the same thing to the trap on the other side of the Laughing Brook. If you're afraid, just say so, and I'll take care of both traps."

Now Bobby Coon *was* afraid, because, you see, he had never had anything to do with traps. But he wasn't willing to own up that he was afraid. He knew that if he showed that he was afraid he never would hear the end of it, for Billy Mink would be sure to tell everybody he knew. He thought the matter over for a few minutes and then he grunted, "I guess if you can do it, I can."

"All right. Let's get busy," cried Billy Mink, jumping up. "I don't want to spend the rest of the night sitting around here."

So Billy Mink swam across the Laughing Brook and Bobby Coon slowly shuffled along on his side down towards the little fence where the trap was set.

Chapter IX

Bobby Coon Gets a Fright

Sense and reason take to flight
In the face of sudden fright.
Billy Mink.

BOBBY Coon walked slowly down the bank of the Laughing Brook to the little fence with the little opening in it where he knew a trap was hidden. Bobby was not at all easy in his mind. He didn't know much about traps. If he had known more about them than he did, he would have been less afraid. Looking across the Laughing Brook he could see a little brown form bounding along the other bank in the moonlight. It was Billy Mink. He knew that Billy was not afraid and that Billy was going to do on that side of the Laughing Brook what he himself had agreed to do on his side.

Bobby approached the little opening in that fence made of sticks and studied it carefully. Billy Mink had said there was a trap there, but look as he would Bobby couldn't see a sign of one. Some wet, dead leaves lay in the little opening in the fence and nothing else was to be seen. Billy Mink had said the trap was under those leaves. Bobby wondered how Billy Mink knew. Billy had told him that there was no danger except right in that little opening.

27

Very cautiously Bobby pulled away the dead
leaves that covered the ground on his side of the
little fence in front of the opening. He even dug down
into the sand a little. Presently his fingers caught
on something hard. He pulled them away as if they
had been burned. Nothing happened. Curiosity gave
Bobby new courage. He dug away very carefully the
leaves and sand at that particular spot and presently
he uncovered something shiny. Anything bright
and shiny always interests Bobby Coon. Again he
touched it and snatched away his paw. Nothing happened. Then Bobby got hold of that shiny thing and
pulled ever so gently. The leaves in the little opening in the fence moved. Bobby pulled again. Those
leaves moved some more. You see, Bobby had hold
of the chain of that hidden trap.

Finding that there was nothing dangerous about
the chain, Bobby continued to pull, and presently
there was the trap itself right in front of him. He sat
down and studied it. He wondered how it worked.
He was afraid of it, but he was very, very curious.
There it lay with its jaws spread wide. Bobby remembered that Billy Mink had said that there would
be no danger if he put his paw under it. Very cautiously Bobby slipped a paw underneath. All of a
sudden that trap jumped right off the ground. There
was a wicked-sounding snap, and those two jaws
flew up and came together so swiftly that Bobby
didn't really see what had happened. He had sprung
the trap.

Bobby didn't wait to see what had happened or what was going to happen next. He almost turned a back somersault in his hurry to get away from that strange thing. He scurried along back up the Laughing Brook as if he expected that trap would follow him.

Chapter X

Billy and Bobby Warn Their Friends

To feel as happy as you would
Try working for the general good.
Billy Mink.

BOBBY Coon had been so frightened when he
had sprung that trap by the Laughing Brook
that probably he would have run clear back to his
home in the Green Forest had he not found Billy
Mink waiting for him at the old log where they had
met earlier in the evening. Billy was grinning.

"What are you running for?" he demanded. "I
thought you were not afraid."

Bobby Coon stopped. "It—it tried to catch me,"
he panted. "It jumped right at me."

Billy Mink chuckled. "But I see it didn't catch you,"
said he. "Didn't I tell you it wouldn't hurt you if you
put your paw under it? That kind of a trap is perfectly harmless as long as you do not step in it. I'm
glad you sprung it. I sprung the one on the other
side of the Laughing Brook the same way. Now, both
of those traps are harmless. They will be until the
trapper sets them again. We can go up and down the
Laughing Brook through the openings in those little
fences with nothing to fear as long as those traps

30

are in plain sight. That trapper will probably come around to-morrow, but for the remainder of to-night there is nothing for us to worry about. Let's go down the Laughing Brook to the Smiling Pool."

The idea of going down to the Smiling Pool was too much for Bobby Coon to resist. So he followed Billy Mink down the bank of the Laughing Brook. When they reached the trap which Bobby had sprung, Billy Mink kicked it aside as he passed. It was plain to see that Billy had known what he had been talking about when he had said that now that trap was perfectly harmless. Then, without hesitating, Billy slipped through the little opening in that fence the trapper had built. That proved there was nothing to fear there now, so Bobby followed. He had to make the opening big enough to get through, but he did this by pulling up a couple of the sticks.

When they reached the Smiling Pool, they saw Little Joe Otter sitting on the Big Rock. Jerry Muskrat was swimming over towards his house.

"Hi, you fellows!" called Billy Mink. "Come over here. We've something to tell you."

Little Joe Otter and Jerry Muskrat had a race over to the place where Billy Mink and Bobby Coon were waiting.

"What is it you have to tell us?" demanded Little Joe. "I don't believe it's anything important."

"That depends on how you look at it," retorted Billy Mink. "Somebody has been setting traps along

Jerry Muskrat was swimming over
towards his house.   *Page 31.*

the Laughing Brook. I've found three of them, and Bobby Coon and I have sprung two of them. We thought we'd just come down here and give you fellows warning." Then Bobby and Billy told Little Joe and Jerry all about those traps.

Chapter XI

Billy and Little Joe Decide to Go Visiting

Don't scoff at one who runs away;
He'll live to scoff at you some day.
Billy Mink.

AFTER visiting the Smiling Pool and warning Little Joe Otter and Jerry Muskrat to watch out for traps, Bobby Coon decided that the Laughing Brook was altogether too dangerous a place for him, so he turned back into the Green Forest, firmly resolved to keep away from the Laughing Brook. Billy Mink and Little Joe Otter talked things over.

"I found three traps," said Billy Mink. "There may be some I have not found. Anyway, it is certain that when that trapper finds that I know about those traps, he will set some more. I don't believe he is smart enough to hide a trap so that we cannot find it. But you know, accidents will happen. He knows that you and I live along the Laughing Brook and he will simply make life miserable for us by continuing to set traps. Do you know what I believe I'll do?"

"What?" asked Little Joe Otter.

"I believe I'll go away for a visit," replied Billy Mink. "I've been feeling rather restless for some time, anyway, and there isn't any better time of year to go visiting than right now, before the snow and ice come.

34

There's a certain brook some distance from here that for a long time I've been thinking of visiting. I believe I'll start tonight and I'll stay long enough for this trapper to get tired of setting traps and catching nothing."

"That's a good idea," said Little Joe Otter. "I believe I'll go visiting myself. I always did like to travel. There is no sense in taking foolish risks, and that is just what we would be doing by staying here. I think I'll go down to the Big River and stay awhile. The fishing here isn't as good as it might be, anyway. I wonder if Jerry Muskrat will go visiting too. Let's tell him what we are going to do and see if he wants to go along with one of us."

"He can't go with me," declared Billy Mink, in a most decided tone. "He travels too slowly. I don't believe he would want to go with me anyway, because, between you and me, I suspect Jerry is a little afraid of me."

Little Joe Otter grinned. "I guess he has reason to be," said he. "I've been told that the Mink family has a liking for Muskrat meat. I hardly think he'll want to go along with me either, because he is such a home-loving body. But anyway, we'll tell him what we're going to do and then he can do as he pleases."

So Billy Mink and Little Joe Otter hunted up Jerry Muskrat and told him how they were going to fool the trapper by going visiting. They urged him to do the same thing.

Chapter XII

Billy Has the Wandering Foot

If to yourself you would be true,
Use all the talents given you.
                                    Billy Mink.

WHEN a person becomes uneasy and cannot settle in one place for any length of time but wants to keep traveling, he is said to be possessed of the wandering foot. This means that he wants to wander about in search of new scenes and new adventures. To put it very plainly, he becomes sort of a tramp.

Billy Mink for some time had felt a desire to go visiting. These traps gave him a real excuse for so doing. So Billy turned his back on the Laughing Brook and started for another brook some distance away. He had not intended to go farther than this brook. But when he got there he found that the fishing was not as good as he had hoped it would be, so he decided to keep on moving until he found a place where food was plentiful and he would be contented for a while.

Now while Billy Mink is a great lover of the water and is almost as much at home in it as Jerry Muskrat, he is equally at home on land. In fact, Billy often wanders long distances from water. He likes variety, and there are times when he would rather hunt than fish. He is a very good hunter, as many a mouse and bird has found out too late. So, leaving the brook where the fishing was poor, Billy started off across country for nowhere in particular. He is one of the most independent of all the little people of the Green Forest and the Green Meadows. He never worries over where the next meal is coming from. He feels quite capable of taking care of himself, wherever he may be. No one understands the art of hiding better than does Billy Mink. He is quick as a flash and the way he can disappear when apparently there is nothing to hide under is astonishing.

So Billy wandered about aimlessly, just having a good time. He traveled mostly at night, though occasionally he became restless during the day and continued his journey then. In the Green Forest he hunted Whitefoot and Mrs. Grouse. In the open meadow land he hunted Meadow Mice. When he came to a brook he went fishing. So, at last, his wanderings brought him to a farmyard. There was a big barn there. Also there was a henhouse containing many hens. Between the henhouse and the barn was a big woodpile. At the sight of that woodpile, Billy grinned. That was just the sort of a place he liked. You know he is so slim that he can slip through very small places, and he knew that in that woodpile he would be quite safe.

"This place looks good to me," said Billy. "I think I'll stay awhile."

Chapter XIII

Billy Makes Himself at Home

Enough to eat, a place to sleep,
A coat to shut out winter's chill—
What more can anybody ask
Their cup of happiness to fill?
Billy Mink.

THE big woodpile between the barn and the henhouse in the farmyard Billy Mink had discovered
was a regular castle for Billy. That is what it was,
a regular castle. Billy is so slim that he could slip
through the openings between the sticks in much
the same way that Striped Chipmunk pops in and
out between the stones of the old stone wall. Billy
doesn't need much room and he soon found that
down underneath that wood were little chambers
plenty big enough for him to curl up in.

The first thing he did was to make himself thoroughly acquainted with that woodpile. He found
every opening that led into or under it. He learned
every little passage it contained. He picked out one
of the best of the little chambers down underneath
in which to sleep when he was tired. No one could
get at him under that woodpile. He felt as safe there
as ever he had felt anywhere in all his life. It made

him chuckle to think how safe he was there, and all the time he would be living right close to those two-legged creatures called men, who delight in killing such little people as Billy.

As soon as he had become thoroughly familiar with that woodpile, Billy set out to explore the surroundings. His new home suited him, but a home without food would be as bad as no home at all. So Billy started out to see what chances there were of making a good living.

First he visited the henhouse. It didn't take him long to find a way under the henhouse and discover a hole in a dark corner of the henhouse floor through which he could slip with ease. But Billy didn't go inside that night. Billy possesses a shrewd little head. He had had experience enough with men to know that it was best for them not to know he was anywhere about. He knew that those hens belonged to men and that the instant they found one killed or missing they would begin to hunt for him. So, though the smell of those hens made Billy's mouth water, he decided that he would see what other food was to be found.

From the henhouse Billy went over to the big barn. This was another place just to his liking. Underneath it was dark, the very kind of a place Billy liked. There were holes up through the floor. Billy sniffed at the edge of the first one he came to and he knew right away who had made that hole.

It had been made by Robber the Rat. Billy's eyes sparkled. It would be much more fun to hunt Robber the Rat and his relatives than to kill stupid, helpless hens.

Chapter XIV

Billy Has Good Hunting

He longest lives who runs away
When danger lurks along the way.
Billy Mink.

BILLY Mink loves to hunt. He is one of the best hunters among the little people of the Green Forest and the Green Meadows. Not even Reddy Fox is a better hunter than Billy Mink. In the first place, Billy has a wonderful nose. He can follow the scent of a Mouse quite as well as can Reddy Fox. Then, too, Billy possesses sharp ears.

The instant Billy caught the scent of Robber the Rat at the edge of the hole in the floor of that barn, he forgot all about the hens over in the henhouse. He popped up through the hole on to the barn floor and his nose found the scent of Robber the Rat stronger than ever. Billy began to follow it just as Bowser the Hound follows the scent of Reddy Fox. It led straight over to a grain bin. Just as Billy reached one end of the grain bin, a big gray Rat, with two others at his heels, scrambled out of the other end of the grain bin and with squeaks of fright scampered away. How they had known of his coming, Billy didn't know. Probably they had smelled him, for Billy has quite a strong scent of his own. Anyway, they had discovered his presence.

With a bound Billy was after them. Almost at once the three Rats separated. Billy didn't hesitate. He followed the largest one. He followed him with his nose; that was all he needed to guide him.

Now that Rat knew every nook and corner and every hiding-place in that big barn. Also he knew that there was no place big enough for him to get into which Billy Mink could not get into too, and fear gave speed to his legs. Behind and under boxes, over grain bins, squeezing through narrow places and racing across open places, the Rat ran, with Billy behind him. At last he was cornered.

Instantly that Rat changed completely. He whirled about and faced Billy Mink, showing savage teeth. He was big and strong and he intended to fight. For just an instant Billy Mink stopped. Now a Rat is quick but Billy Mink is quicker. That Rat was no coward. He fought and he fought hard, but he fought in vain. He could not get those wicked-looking teeth of his into Billy. In less time than it takes to tell it, the fight was over and Billy Mink had his dinner.

Now Billy knew all about Robber the Rat and his relatives. He knew that they were outcasts among all the little people of the Green Forest and the Green Meadows. He knew that not a single thing could be said in their favor. He knew that the Great World would be a better place for everybody if there were no Brown Rats in it.

"There is good hunting here," muttered Billy, as he turned to go back to his new home under the wood-pile. "As long as there is such good hunting here in this barn, I'll keep away from the henhouse." Then he went home and curled up for a nap.

Chapter XV

A Den of Robbers

Greed and Selfishness are twins
Who lead the way to greater sins.
Billy Mink.

WHEN Billy Mink started to explore the big
barn in the farmyard where he had decided
to stay for a while, he didn't know that he was entering a den of robbers. But that is what he was doing. Yes, Sir, that is just what he was doing. You see,
that barn was the home of ever and ever so many of
the tribe of Robber the Rat, and each one of them,
big and little, was a robber. They lived by robbing,
which, you know, is another name for stealing.

Now those robbers had lived in that big barn so
long that they had come to look on it as belonging to
them. They knew every nook and corner and cranny
in it and under it. The farmer who owned it had tried
his best to kill them or drive them away. But those
robber Rats simply laughed at all his efforts. They
were smart. Oh, yes, indeed, they were smart. Robbers often are quite as smart as honest people. They
were too smart for that farmer.

All those Rats belonged to the Brown Rat tribe.
Not that they were all brown. The fact is, the older

ones were quite gray. But that was because they were old and had grown gray with age.

Not all Rats are bad. There is Trader the Wood Rat. He is honest and respected by his neighbors. But all the Brown Rat tribe are outcasts, despised by all the little people of the Green Meadows and the Green Forest, and hated by man. There is no good in them. They become robbers as soon as they can run about, and they remain robbers as long as they live. There is not an honest hair on one of them. They hate the sunlight, for their deeds are deeds of darkness. They are savage.

But with all this, they are clever, very clever, indeed. They are so clever that, in spite of all man's efforts to kill them, their tribe has increased until it is probably the largest tribe of little people who wear fur in all the world, excepting the Mouse tribe.

The farmer who owned that barn had set traps of many kinds, but the wise old leader of the Rats had found each trap and warned all his relatives. The farmer had tried to poison them, but somehow their wise old leader always knew where the poison was and warned them against it. A Cat had been brought to catch them, but the tough old fighters among the Rats had driven that Cat out.

So the Rats had increased, and the greater the numbers, the more they stole. They gnawed holes wherever there was a chance of getting food. They got into the farmer's house and did great damage there. In the spring they had killed young chickens in the henhouse. They stole eggs. In fact, these robbers did as they pleased, and the big barn was their den.

Chapter XVI

A Robber Meeting

To judge another by his size
Is, to say the least, unwise.
Billy Mink.

IT was night in the big barn. It was the night after
Billy Mink's visit, when he had killed the big Rat
there. As soon as Billy had left the barn, the gray
old leader of the Rats had sent word around that
all the Rats in the barn should meet him at once at
their usual meeting-place under the floor.

As soon as the word was received, each member
of the robber band hurried to the meeting-place.
They knew why the gray old leader had called them
together, and as they hurried to the meeting-place,
there was fear in the heart of each of them. It was
long since fear had been known in the big barn. It
was the first time some of them ever had experi-
enced fear. You see, they had been so well taught
how to avoid traps and poison that they did not fear
those things. They had made the Cat afraid of them,
so they did not fear the Cat. It was no trouble at all
to keep out of the way of the farmer, so they did not
fear the farmer.

But this slim, brown enemy who had entered their
den so boldly, and had run down and killed one of

47

their number, had brought fear with him. So, as from every direction the Rats scurried to that meeting-place, they continually looked behind them for that slim, brown creature who moved so swiftly and from whom even their gray old leader had run away. Most of them did not know who Billy Mink was, for they had always lived in that big barn, and no one at all like Billy had ever been there before.

As soon as all the Rats had answered his call, the gray old leader began to speak. "I have called this meeting," said he, "to decide what we had best do. A terrible enemy has come among us, and, as you know, has killed one of our number. He has left the big barn, as I know, because I watched him. For the time being we are quite safe. But when he again becomes hungry, he will return."

"Who is he?" squeaked a young Rat. "He didn't look very big to me. If we all get together, I don't see why we should be afraid of him. We drove out that Cat, and that Cat is a great deal bigger than this fellow. Who is he, anyway?"

"He is Billy Mink," replied the gray old leader gravely.

"And who is Billy Mink?" squeaked another half-grown young robber.

"He is sure death to any Rat he may start out to catch," replied the old leader. "He belongs to the Weasel family, and all members of this family are enemies of the Rat tribe and more to be feared than any other enemy we have."

"He is Billy Mink," replied the gray old
leader gravely.   *Page 48*.

"Why can't we hide when he comes?" asked another young robber. "I never have seen any one I couldn't hide from."

"Then, unless I am greatly mistaken, you are likely to have a chance," snapped the leader.

Chapter XVII

The Robbers Decide to Fight

A bad name sticks as naught else can
To bird or beast or boy or man.
Billy Mink.

WHEN one of the young robber Rats at the meeting of all the Rats in the big barn boasted that he never had seen any one he couldn't hide from, all the other young Rats nodded their heads in approval. You see, they prided themselves on knowing every hiding-place in that big barn, and they never had known an enemy small enough to follow them to these hiding-places. When the gray old leader of that robber gang said that unless he was greatly mistaken they were likely to have a chance to see some one they couldn't hide from, they at once demanded to know what he meant.

The old leader looked around the circle of Rats waiting for him to speak. There were big Rats, little Rats, and middle-sized Rats. There were Rats gray with age, and sleek, brown-coated Rats. He counted noses. Every Rat of the tribe, save only the babies too small to leave the nests, and the one whom Billy Mink had caught, was present. In the faces of the gray old Rats he could see worry. Like himself, they understood the danger they were in. In the faces of

51

the younger Rats there was no worry. It was plain to see that they felt quite confident of being able to take care of themselves. Never in all their lives had they met an enemy they could not run away from, and he knew they didn't believe such an enemy lived.

"Knowledge of life is obtained only through experience," he began. "You who are so sure you can hide from this new enemy are confident because you are ignorant. Cats and Dogs you do not fear, because you can go where they cannot follow. But this Mink who has found our den can follow where any of you, even the smallest, can go."

"But if he does not see us hide, how can he find us?" squeaked a sharp-nosed young Rat.

"A Mink does not have to see in order to follow," retorted the gray old leader. "You cannot move without leaving a scent which he can follow by means of his wonderful nose. All he has to do is to find where you have been and then follow straight to where you are hiding. He can run faster than you can and longer than you can. There is no escape from him once he sets out to catch one of you. The best fighter among us is no match for him alone. I tell you, friends, our tribe is in danger. It is in the greatest danger it ever has faced. I have called you together to make this plain to you and to get your ideas as to what we should do."

For a few moments no one spoke. The worried look on the faces of the older Rats had crept into the faces of the younger Rats. Finally a scarred old fighter spoke.

"It seems to me," said he, "there is only one thing to do, and that is, fight. What one of us alone cannot do, all of us together can. I propose that the next time this enemy appears, we all attack him together."

To this all the Rats agreed.

Chapter XVIII

The Rats Plan to Kill Billy Mink

An idle boaster, it is clear,
Is he who says he knows no fear.
Billy Mink.

IT having been agreed by all the Rats in the big barn that they would stand by each other and all attack Billy Mink at once, the next time he appeared, they immediately began to feel better. Only the oldest ones shook their heads doubtfully and continued to look worried. The younger ones boasted. Had they not driven away the Cat which the farmer had put in the barn to catch them? And was not the Cat very much bigger than this new enemy? They began to talk among themselves of the fun they would have when Billy Mink should next appear.

"I'm not afraid," said one.

"Nor I," cried another. And all the rest of the young Rats boasted in the same way.

But the gray old leader still shook his head and looked worried. "It is all very well for you to brag of what you will do," said he. "But bragging never yet won a battle. If we would keep our homes here in this big barn, where many of you have spent your lives, we must make our plans to kill this terrible enemy. It will not do to simply drive him away, for he might return when least expected. Always there must be two or three on watch. The instant that Mink appears, warning must be given, and then all of us fall on him at once. As I told you before, the best fighter among us would be helpless if he had to face that fellow alone. But if we all attack him together, there will be nothing to fear."

So certain of the sharpest-eyed Rats were appointed to watch all the holes through which Billy Mink might enter the big barn. When it should become necessary for them to go hunt for food, other Rats were to take their places. All the others scattered to their homes. Some lived under the barn, some lived on the main floor of the barn, and some lived in the hay loft. The old Rats were still worried, but the younger ones were filled with pleasant excitement. They rather hoped that Billy Mink would come soon. They wanted to show how brave they could be. Not a doubt crept into the mind of one of them that all would end as they had planned.

Meanwhile Billy Mink was comfortably dreaming in the little chamber he had chosen under the big woodpile between the big barn and the henhouse. Billy's dreams were pleasant dreams. That is, they were pleasant dreams for him. He dreamed he was hunting Rats. Yes, they were very pleasant dreams for Billy. But had any of the Rats in the big barn had those dreams, they would have been anything but pleasant. It is funny how in this world the things which are very pleasant for one are very unpleasant for another.

Chapter XIX

The Danger Signal

The evil-minded fear the light,
But love the darkness of the night.
Billy Mink.

THERE was a great deal of uneasiness in the big barn where the robber Rats lived. Would Billy Mink return or had he just made a chance visit and gone on somewhere else? The gray old leader of the Rats felt sure that Billy would return. He was too anxious to eat, and you know when a Rat's appetite fails he must be very much disturbed indeed.

But the younger Rats thought the gray old leader needlessly frightened, and they went about their business of stealing food and gnawing holes wherever there seemed a chance of finding a new food supply, just as if nothing had happened. However, each hole which led into the barn was continually watched by sharp eyes. Those Rats did not intend to be taken by surprise a second time.

Rats prefer the hours of darkness. They hate the light of day. Perhaps that is because their deeds are deeds of darkness. So, when daylight came, most of the Rats returned to their beds to sleep. Only underneath the barn, where it was dark, did any of them continue to run about, seeking what mischief they might get into. But the wise, gray old leader saw to it that a watch was kept on each hole just the same as during the night. He didn't think Billy Mink would come in the daytime, but he was wise enough to know that Billy Mink is forever doing the unexpected. He suspected that Billy would take great pains not to let the farmer who owned that barn know that he was anywhere about. "He'll probably sleep all day," thought the gray old leader, "but just as soon as it begins to get dark he'll be back here. I just feel it in my bones."

But it wasn't dark when there suddenly sounded the danger signal from one of the watchers. In fact, it was broad daylight, the very middle of the day. You see, daylight and darkness are all one to Billy Mink. He sleeps whenever he feels sleepy, regardless of whether it be night or day. At all other times he is very wide-awake indeed.

It happened that Billy had wakened just about noon that day, and as is usual with him, after a nap, he was hungry. If he had been a Rat instead of a Mink, he might have remained under the woodpile until darkness came. But Billy is very sure of his ability to take care of himself. He first made sure that no one was about. Then he slipped out from under that pile of wood and a minute later he was under the barn. Then it was that the danger signal was sounded by the Rat who was watching the hole through which Billy entered. It was at once passed on from Rat to Rat, until every one in the barn knew that their enemy had returned.

Chapter XX

Why the Plans of the Rats Failed

Beware the coward and the sneak;
He dares to face none but the weak.
Billy Mink.

YOU remember that the Rats in the big barn
had agreed that if Billy Mink should return,
they would all attack him at once and kill him or so
frighten him that he would leave and never return.
It was a perfectly good plan. Billy was more than a
match for any single Rat. He might be more than a
match for any two Rats. But if he had to fight all the
Rats at once, he wouldn't have the smallest chance
in the world.

Those Rats had been very bold and brave when
they had met to plan how they should get rid of this
new enemy. Especially bold and brave had been the
younger Rats. They had agreed that the instant they
heard the signal, they would rush to do their part in
the attack on Billy Mink.

Only the wise, gray old leader had been doubtful.
He had not let the others know that he was doubtful, for this would not have done at all. But he knew
what the younger Rats did not know, which was
that born in every Rat is great fear of all members
of Billy Mink's family—a fear so great that when it

is aroused all else is forgotten. He knew that such fear becomes terror, and terror destroys courage. It makes cowards of even those who are thought to be brave. So the gray old leader was doubtful, and that doubt increased the fear with which the very thought of Billy Mink filled him.

Now the gray old leader was not a coward himself. He would never have become a leader if he had been a coward. When he heard that dreaded danger signal, he scrambled out of the nest where he had been taking a nap and hurried forth to lead his tribe in the great fight they had planned. Almost at once he met one of the loudest boasters amongst the younger Rats, and this fellow was running in the opposite direction from the way he should have been going. More than this, he was squealing with fright. Then another and another and still another raced frantically past, each squealing with terror. He could not stop them. They were frantic with fear and gave him no heed.

In all directions he could hear frightened squeaks and squeals and the scampering of many feet. He knew then that what he had most feared had happened. The mere presence of Billy Mink had awakened that inborn fear, and each Rat was thinking only of himself and how he could escape. Sadly the old leader turned and fled to save his own life. He knew that their plans for getting rid of Billy Mink had failed and that he never would be able to make the other Rats stand and fight.

Chapter XXI

The Rats Leave the Big Barn

There's nothing quite like fear to spread
And wrap the whole Great World in dread.
Billy Mink.

BILLY Mink's second visit to the big barn had
been an occasion of great pleasure to Billy and
terror to all the Rats who lived there. He had hunted
them just for the pleasure of hearing their squeals
of fright and the scampering of their feet, as they
raced this way and that way, seeking safety. With his
wonderful nose he had followed them to their most
secret hiding-places. Three he had caught, and he
could have caught more had he really wanted to.

When he had become tired of the hunt, Billy had
curled up for a nap in a corner of the haymow where
it was dark and quiet. He had done this instead of
going back to the woodpile. It was very comfortable
there. Besides, it would be very handy to be right
there when he felt like hunting again.

It wasn't long before all the Rats knew just where
Billy was. One of them had happened to pass near
enough to smell Billy and had at once passed the
word along to all the others.

"Now is the time," said the wise old leader, "for us

to get together and attack him. Who will join with me?"

Not a single Rat came forward. The gray old leader shook his head sadly. "You are cowards, all of you," said he. "If you will not fight, there is just one thing left for us to do."

"What is that?" squeaked one of the young Rats who had been loudest in his boasting before Billy Mink had appeared the second time.

"We've got to leave this barn," replied the gray old leader. "If we remain here, it will be to die. That Mink will stay here, or if he doesn't, he will keep coming back until he has hunted down and killed every Rat. We must leave the barn and do it at once. There is no time to be lost. Probably he is asleep now. By the time he awakes, we must be out of this barn. The Rat who doesn't leave it now never will leave it."

Immediately there was a great discussion. Every Rat there knew that the wise old leader was right. But where should they go? It was winter, and they could not live long out of doors. They must go to a place where they would find both shelter and food. They might as well remain to be killed by Billy Mink as to go forth and starve or freeze to death. At least that is what some of them said. Some suggested one thing and some another. Finally they turned to the gray old leader for his advice. They had followed him so long that they had learned to trust to his wisdom.

The rats leave the big barn.　*Page 63.*

Chapter XXII

Billy Mink's Surprise

A cause there is that will explain
A mystery, and make it plain.
Billy Mink.

BILLY Mink opened his eyes. At first he couldn't think where he was. Everything about him was strange. Then, all in a flash, it came to him where he was. He was in a dark corner of the haymow in the big barn where the Rats lived.

Billy yawned. Then he stretched one leg and then another. He yawned again, stretched some more, then lay quiet for a few minutes, trying to decide whether to take another nap or hunt those Rats again.

"I may as well learn all about this barn while I am here," thought Billy. "One never knows when such knowledge may come in very handy. Besides, I want to find out where all these Rats live. How they did squeal and squeak, when they discovered me!" Billy chuckled at the memory. "It is great fun to hunt them."

Billy lazily got to his feet and arched his back, which was one way of stretching. Then he started out to explore the big barn. Of course he didn't go far before he smelled a Rat. That is to say, he smelled

65

the scent left by the feet of a Rat. Right away Billy forgot everything but the fun of hunting, the game of hide-and-seek in which death was the price of being caught. He started out along the trail of that Rat. By and by, way down under some boxes, he came to a nest. It was made of old rags, torn paper, and other bits of rubbish. Billy didn't knock to find out if any one were at home. No, indeed, Billy didn't knock. He just popped his head right in. He expected to find some babies at home if no one else, because he knew that there are babies most of the time in the home of a Rat.

Right then, Billy got his first surprise. That nest was empty! Yes, sir, it was empty! There had been babies there, as his nose told him, but they had been carried away. Billy hunted about a bit until he found the trail leading away from the nest. This he followed. It led him downstairs to a hole in the barn floor, through this to the ground, and straight to an opening which led out of doors.

"Huh!" muttered Billy. "This is queer." He ran about a bit and it didn't take him long to discover that there were many tracks leading to that opening out of doors. He could tell by the smell that those Rats had gone out and not come back.

"It looks as if my future dinners have run away," muttered Billy, and then he began to explore that barn in earnest. There wasn't a hole or crevice or cranny in it that he didn't poke his nose into. There wasn't a Rat nest that he didn't find. But not a glimpse of a single Rat did he get, not the squeak of a single voice did he hear. There wasn't a Rat in the barn! When he had gone to sleep there had been many. He had heard them squeaking all about him. Do you wonder that he was surprised?

Chapter XXIII

Billy Hunts in Vain

All secrets, 'tis the law of fate,
Will be discovered soon or late.
Billy Mink.

IN vain Billy Mink searched for Rats in the big barn.
The smell of them was everywhere, but the Rats
themselves had disappeared completely. Time after
time, following a trail, Billy was led to the opening
out of doors under the barn. It was clear that all the
Rats had left the big barn, and that all had gone out
the same way.

"They've moved off somewhere," thought Billy. "I
frightened them so that they didn't dare stay here
any longer. All have gone, young, old, big, little, and
middle-sized. There is no fun left for me here in the
big barn. I think I'll follow them. Where they can go,
I can go. They are a gang of robbers. They are ugly,
dirty, and of no account whatever. In fact, they're
worse than that. They have so many babies at a
time, and have them so often, that there is danger
that they will drive their honest neighbors off the
earth. Yes, I think I'll follow them."

Billy cautiously poked his head through the opening that led out of doors. Then he blinked with surprise. Outside everything was spotlessly white. It

was snowing. It had been snowing for some time. Not a footprint of a single Rat was to be seen. Moreover, there was no scent for Billy to follow by means of his wonderful nose. The snow had covered their trail. Billy could only lick his lips and wonder in which direction those Rats had gone.

"If I knew more about this part of the country, I would know better where to look for those Rats," muttered Billy. "As it is, I haven't been here long enough to know about anything but this barn, the henhouse, and the big woodpile between the two. I wonder if they can have moved over to that woodpile or to the henhouse. The woodpile would give them hiding-places, but they wouldn't find anything to eat there. If they have gone to the henhouse, they can hide underneath it and for food they can steal eggs and perhaps kill a hen. I've known Rats to do just those things. I've known them to kill chickens and then have the owner of the chickens blame me or Jimmy Skunk for it. I hate Rats. Everybody else does. I know nearly everybody, and I don't know a single person who has a good word to say for Robber the Rat and his gang. I think I'll run over to the henhouse to see if they are there."

So Billy Mink went first to the big woodpile and from there to the henhouse, but not so much as the smell of a Rat did he find in either place.

Chapter XXIV

Where the Rats Were

The mischievous will find some day
That for their mischief they must pay.
Billy Mink.

IF Billy Mink didn't know where the Rats who had left the big barn had gone to, the farmer who owned the big barn and the henhouse and the wood-pile knew. Yes, indeed, the farmer and his family knew just where those Rats were. They were in the farmhouse!

You see, the wise, gray old leader of the Rats knew that the safest place for them was in that farmhouse. In the first place it was big, and that meant that there was plenty of room with ever and ever so many hiding-places. There was food there, plenty of it, to be stolen. They could be very comfortable in that farmhouse. More than this, they would be safe from Billy Mink. That gray old leader knew that Billy Mink would hesitate a long time about actually entering the house, because of his fear of man. He didn't believe that Billy would dream of looking for them in that house, especially if he couldn't track them over there. This Billy couldn't do, as the wise old leader very well knew, because it had been snowing when

70

the Rats left the big barn, and the falling snow had covered their tracks and destroyed the scent.

So, while Billy Mink was looking under the wood-pile and in the henhouse for those Rats, they were making themselves very much at home in the farm-house. They could climb about between the walls and go where they pleased. The first thing to do was to make homes for the babies. It didn't take some of those Rats long to find the way to the attic. Now the attic was filled with trunks and boxes and papers and all sorts of odds and ends. It was just such a place as Rats love. Right away the mother Rats be-gan to tear up papers and make rags of clothing that hung in the attic. Rags and paper make the finest kind of a nest for a Rat. These nests they hid in dark places behind boxes and trunks.

And while they were busy with this, the father Rats set out to search for food. It didn't take them long to find the pantry and gnaw holes through the wall into it. And they were not quiet about their work, either. The farmer and the farmer's wife knew what was going on. They could hear the scamper of little feet across the attic floor and faint squeaks.

"Gracious!" exclaimed the farmer. "I should think all the Rats in the barn had moved over here." He little guessed how exactly he had hit on the truth.

Chapter XXV

The Farmer and His Wife Are in Despair

A pity 'tis, but it is true,
The innocent must suffer too.
Billy Mink.

THE farmer who owned the big barn where the Rats had lived was puzzled. After a few days he became sure that there wasn't a Rat left in the big barn. He knew that they had all moved over to the farmhouse. They had been bad enough when they had lived in the big barn, but they were ever so much worse living in the house. He knew that Rats did not move like this without a cause. This meant that they must have been driven out of the big barn, and who or what could have driven them out was more than the farmer could guess. For years he had tried to get rid of the Rats there and hadn't been able to. Now suddenly they had deserted the big barn and taken possession of his house.

"I wish," said the farmer, "I could find out what drove those Rats over here. Then perhaps I could use the same means to drive them out of the house."

"I wish you could," replied his wife. "I don't know what we're going to do. Those Rats are getting so bold that they don't pay any attention to me at all. They run across the pantry floor in broad daylight.

The only way I can keep food safe from them is in tin cans or earthen jars with covers, and they have even managed to get the covers off of some of these. They get in the flour barrel. They have spoiled the milk. They have stolen the eggs. In fact, there isn't anything they haven't gotten into. They keep me awake nights by their squealing and racing about through the walls. They're getting so bold that I am afraid of them."

So the farmer set all his traps. He set traps in the attic and in the pantry and in the woodshed. He put poisoned food where he was sure the Rats would find it. But it was all in vain. Those Rats had learned all about traps, and the gray old leader of them had learned to be suspicious of food left where it was easy to get. He warned the other Rats not to touch this food. The farmer blocked up the holes in the pantry walls, but as fast as he blocked them up, the Rats gnawed new ones.

So it was that the farmer and his wife were in despair. Do what they would, they couldn't get rid of those Rats. The Rats got into the cellar and stole the vegetables. It got so the farmer's wife didn't dare go down cellar. She was afraid of being bitten by a Rat, and you know the bite of a Rat often is poisonous.

Chapter XXVI

The Rats Start A Fire

A tiny spark, once it is free,
An awful thing may grow to be.
Billy Mink.

RATS are born thieves. They not only steal food, but they carry off many other things, things for which they really have no use at all. Now it happened that one of the young Rats in the farmhouse found some matches and took them to his nest under the floor of the shed. There, having nothing else to do, he nibbled at them to see what the queer stuff on the ends of them might be. His sharp teeth caused one of them to light, and of course that instantly lighted all the rest of them. With a squeak of fright the Rat ran away, for like all the little people of the Green Forest and the Green Meadows, a Rat fears the Red Terror, which we call fire, more than anything else.

Now that Rat's nest was made chiefly of chewed-up paper and old rags. Nothing could have been better for the Red Terror. It blazed up instantly. The floor just above was of very, very dry wood, for the boards of that floor had been there many years. In no time at all that shed was afire.

All the Rats under the floor fled in terror into the house. Smoke began to pour out of the open door of the shed. The farmer at work in the barnyard saw it and ran as fast as he could to try to put the fire out.

For a while the farmer and his wife had a hard fight with the Red Terror. They pumped water as fast as ever they could and carried it in pails to throw on the fire. At first it looked as if the Red Terror would be too much for them and their house would be burned up, but after a while the water was too much for the Red Terror and drowned it out.

"Whew!" exclaimed the farmer, as he and his wife sat down to rest for a moment. "That was a narrow escape. How under the sun could that fire have started?"

"I haven't the least idea," replied his wife. "I was upstairs at the time. There wasn't a thing in that shed which could have started it. Do you suppose that anybody could have set it?"

The farmer shook his head. "No," said he, "that fire started under the floor." Then a sudden thought came to him. "I know how it started!" he cried angrily. "It was those pesky Rats. It was those pesky Rats, as sure as I live. They must have found some matches somewhere and taken them to a nest under the floor. Then, while they were nibbling at them, they set one going. We've got to get rid of those Rats or we won't have a house left over our heads. I don't know how we're going to do it, but we've got to get rid of those Rats."

Chapter XXVII

Billy Is Discovered

Before you act be sure you know
That what you think is really so.
Billy Mink.

AFTER the Rats left the big barn, Billy Mink found it less easy to get plenty to eat. There were Mice in the big barn, and for several days Billy managed to catch enough of these to keep from going hungry. But Mice can get into places too small for Billy to follow, and those that were left soon learned to keep out of his way.

Then Billy's thoughts turned to the hens in the henhouse. He had not intended to kill any of those hens, because he knew that as soon as he did, the farmer who owned them would hunt for him, and then he would have to move on. He was so comfortably located in the woodpile that he was not anxious to move on. But one must eat, and now that the Rats had disappeared and the Mice had learned to keep out of his way, Billy's thoughts turned to those hens.

It was the very night after the fire which the Rats had started in the back shed of the farmhouse that Billy made up his mind to have a chicken dinner. He slipped under the henhouse and up through a hole in the corner which he already knew about. All the hens were roosting high, fast asleep with their heads under their wings. Had Reddy Fox been in Billy Mink's place, he would have been somewhat puzzled as to how he might catch one of those hens. But Billy wasn't puzzled, not a bit of it. You see, Billy can climb almost like a Squirrel. Reddy Fox would have had to jump, and probably would have awakened and frightened the whole flock. Billy Mink simply climbed up to one of the roosts, stole along it to the nearest hen, and with one quick snap of his stout little jaws, he killed that hen without even waking her.

Now, had Billy's cousin, Shadow the Weasel, been in his place, he would have gone right on killing those hens from sheer love of killing. But Billy Mink killed that hen simply because he must have something to eat, and one hen was more than enough to furnish him a dinner. When he had finished his dinner, he went back to his snug bed under the big woodpile.

Of course, when the farmer came out to feed the hens in the morning he discovered what had happened. He didn't know who had killed that hen, but he knew that it must have been some one very small to have gotten into the henhouse. He hunted about until he found the hole in the dark corner. He knew that that hole had been made by a Rat, and at first he thought it must have been Rats who killed that hen and this increased his anger.

That afternoon he happened to look out of the barn door towards the woodpile, and he was just in time to see a slim, brown form whisk out of sight under the wood.

"Ha, ha!" exclaimed the farmer. "Now I know who the thief is. There is a Mink in that woodpile. He is the fellow who killed that hen last night. I think, Mr. Mink, we'll make you pay for that hen with your brown coat."

Chapter XXVIII

The Farmer Guesses the Truth

Who heeds a warning proves he's wise,
And guards himself against surprise.
Billy Mink.

IF Billy Mink had known that he had been discovered by the farmer, under whose woodpile he was living, it is probable that he would have moved on in search of new adventures just as soon as the Black Shadows had crept out across the barnyard that night. But Billy didn't know. He had been living there so comfortably that he had grown a little careless, otherwise he never would have ventured out in broad daylight.

That night he decided he would have another chicken for dinner, so he ran over to the henhouse, intending to slip through the hole in the dark corner, just as he had done the night before. But the minute Billy had poked his nose through that hole, he knew something was wrong. There was a queer smell. Billy tested it very carefully with his nose. It was the man smell. That was enough to make Billy suspicious. In less time than it takes to tell it, he had found a trap in that henhouse, so placed that he couldn't possibly get in through that hole without stepping in it. Right away Billy decided that he didn't care for a chicken dinner that night. He would go back to the big barn and try to catch a mouse.

Now, when the farmer had first discovered Billy Mink, his one thought had been to catch Billy. He knew that Billy's brown coat could be sold for enough to pay several times over for the hen Billy had killed. So he had set a trap in the henhouse. That night the Rats in the house were noisier than ever. For a while he forgot Billy Mink, trying to think of some way to get rid of those Rats. Then his thoughts came back to Billy Mink, and all in a flash he understood why those Rats had deserted the big barn and come over to the house.

"It was that Mink!" he exclaimed, right out loud.

"What are you talking about?" demanded his wife.

"That Mink I saw to-day going under the woodpile, the one who killed the chicken last night," replied the farmer. "That fellow must have been living around here for some time, and he chased those Rats out of the barn. There isn't a doubt about it. He hunted those Rats in the barn until he frightened them so they moved over here. You see, he could follow them everywhere, and there was no getting away from him. The pesky robbers simply decided they had got to move and our house was the best place to move to.

"It's all as plain as the nose on my face. If the rats had remained in the barn, I don't believe that Mink would have bothered the chickens. Probably he doesn't dare come over here to the house, or else he doesn't know where the Rats went to. If he would just come over here for a while, we would soon be rid of those pests, and I would forgive him for killing that hen."

Chapter XXIX

The Farmer Makes Friends with Billy

Friendship is most surely won
By kindly deeds for others done.
Billy Mink.

THE farmer did a lot of thinking after he guessed that it was Billy Mink who had driven all the Rats out of his barn into his house. "If I could get that little brown rascal over here to the house," thought the farmer, "I would soon be rid of those robber Rats. But how am I going to do it? If he doesn't know that those Rats are over here, he certainly will not venture any nearer to the house than that woodpile. And if he cannot get into the henhouse to steal my chickens, he won't stay around here very long, because he will have little to eat. The thing for me to do is see that he has plenty to eat and learns where it comes from."

So the very first thing the farmer did the next morning was to put some scraps of fresh meat just outside the woodpile. It didn't take Billy Mink long to find them. Of course the farmer was out of sight. He was in the barn, peeping through a crack. He saw Billy come out from under the wood and sniff at the pieces of meat. It was clear that Billy was suspicious. He went all around those scraps of meat, and the farmer could tell by the way he moved that Billy suspected a trap.

But Billy found no trap. Of course not, because there was no trap. At last he ventured to seize one of those scraps of meat and darted back into the wood-pile with it. A few minutes later he was out again, just as cautious as before. So, one by one, he took the scraps of meat under the woodpile. The farmer smiled as he saw the last scrap disappear. He knew that Billy had enough for a good meal and that with a stomach well filled he would probably take a nap.

This is just what Billy did. All the time he kept wondering about those scraps of meat and how they had happened to be so handy. "It's queer," thought Billy, "how that meat happened to be right there. I wonder if that farmer could have dropped it. If he did, I hope he'll do it again." With this, Billy went to sleep.

Just at dusk Billy awoke. He was hungry again. He began to think of those hens over in the henhouse. Then he remembered the trap he had found over there and decided he would keep away from the henhouse. He decided that he would go over to the big barn to see if any of those Rats had returned. And then, all of a sudden, he remembered the easy breakfast he had had that morning. Instantly Billy popped his head out from under the woodpile. He didn't really expect to find any more scraps of meat, and you can guess just how surprised and pleased he was when he found that there were some more scraps just where he had found his breakfast that morning. For the first time Billy suspected that they might have been put there especially for him, and in his heart he began to have a friendly feeling for that farmer.

Chapter XXX

Billy Lives High

Misunderstandings cleared away
Bring peace and happiness to stay.
Billy Mink.

BILLY Mink was living high. Yes, sir, Billy Mink was living high. For the first time in his life he didn't have to hunt for his meals. Whenever he became hungry, all he had to do was to slip out from under the woodpile—and there was a meal waiting for him. Of course it hadn't taken Billy long to find out where those meals came from. After the first day Billy had watched. Peeping out from his hiding-place under the wood, he had seen the farmer come from the house and leave something for him to eat, and then go on to feed the hens.

Sometimes Billy would find scraps of meat. Sometimes it would be a piece of fish. Once, when the farmer and his wife had had a chicken dinner, Billy found a couple of chicken heads, of which he is very fond. Always it was something Billy liked. He was living so high that he was actually growing fat and lazy.

And as the days went on, Billy grew less and less afraid of that farmer. He decided that no one who meant harm to him would be so good to him. So after

85

Sometimes Billy would find scraps of meat.   *Page 85.*

a while Billy would come out in broad daylight. In fact, the farmer would have gone hardly ten steps away before Billy would be out to see what had been left for him. And the farmer, on his part, took the greatest care not to do anything to frighten Billy. In short, Billy and the farmer were becoming very good friends.

Just for exercise Billy would occasionally run over to the big barn and hunt for mice. Once he visited the henhouse and found that no longer was there a hole by which he could get into the henhouse. The farmer had blocked up the hole through which Billy had once entered. After he discovered this, Billy kept away from the henhouse. He knew that it was of no use to go there. You see, he is not like the Rats; he doesn't gnaw holes. He makes use of holes some one else has made. His teeth are not made for gnawing.

But Billy wasn't especially disappointed because he couldn't get into the henhouse. In fact, he seldom thought about chickens. You see, he had plenty to eat, and having plenty there was no temptation to try to kill a chicken. So Billy felt very much at home and worried about nothing at all. There was nothing to worry about. He felt as if he quite belonged in that farmyard. Yes, sir, that is how he felt.

Chapter XXXI

Billy Trails His Breakfast

Thoughtful kindness in the end
Is bound to win for you a friend.
Billy Mink.

BILLY Mink had overslept. This was very unusual for Billy. Usually he was watching for the farmer to bring him his breakfast. But this morning Billy had overslept. He knew it the minute his eyes opened. Right away he scrambled out to see what had been left him for breakfast. He found nothing.

He blinked two or three times, for he had become so used to finding his breakfast right at the edge of the woodpile, that he couldn't believe there was none left for him that morning. But there wasn't a thing. Not even the tiniest scrap. Billy began to wonder if some one had stolen his breakfast while he slept.

Right away he put his nose to the ground and began to run about, this way and that way. He was trying to find out if something had been put down and then taken away. He knew that if anything had been there he would be able to smell it, for he has a very wonderful little nose.

Presently a very delicious smell tickled that wonderful little nose. That is, it was a very wonderful smell to Billy. It wouldn't have been wonderful to you. You would have called it a very bad smell. It was the smell of fish, and not fresh fish at that.

Billy began to gallop along with his nose to the ground, following that smell. He didn't care who saw him. You see, he had become so at home in that farmyard that he felt quite safe there. He and the farmer had become very good friends. There was no dog to fear, and Billy wasn't afraid of the Cat. He had just one thought in his mind, and that was to find out what had become of that fish. He was sure it had been meant for him. Whoever had taken it away had dragged it along the ground, and so it was easy for Billy to follow the smell.

He was trailing his breakfast in just the same way he had followed the Rats in the barn. Straight across the barnyard the trail led and over to the shed at the back of the house. There, just in front of a hole under the shed, Billy found the fish. His eyes sparkled and he wasted no time. He began to eat that fish at once. He didn't stop to wonder who had dragged it there. He didn't care. It was his fish, and he intended to make sure of it.

When he had finished the last scrap, Billy felt so stuffed that he didn't want to move any more than he had to. He looked over to the woodpile, and then he looked at the hole under the shed. The woodpile was too far away. He felt sure that he would find a nice comfortable dark place under that shed. Without hesitating a second, he disappeared in the hole.

Chapter XXXII

Billy Makes a Discovery

Keep at whate'er you once begin;
It is the only way to win.
Billy Mink.

WHEN Billy Mink slipped through the hole under the floor of the shed at the back of the farmer's house, his one thought was to find a comfortable place for a nap. He found it without any trouble. You know Billy is not fussy, and he can curl up and sleep almost anywhere. He had stuffed himself so with that fish he had found just outside the hole that he had felt too lazy to explore. So he picked out the first comfortable-looking place he came to and curled up for a nap.

When Billy awoke, he couldn't at first remember where he was. Then he recalled the fish and how he had slipped in under the shed floor.

"Now I am here, I may as well find out all about this place," thought Billy, and got to his feet. He yawned and stretched and then began to run around underneath the floor of the shed, using his nose as he always does. In no time at all a familiar scent tickled his nose.

"Ah, ha!" exclaimed Billy Mink. "So this is where

those Rats came when they left the big barn. I'm not hungry, but I certainly would enjoy a good hunt. I haven't hunted anything bigger than a mouse for ever so long."

Away raced Billy, with his nose to the ground, following the scent of a Rat. It didn't take him long to find a nest under the shed floor. But there was no one in that nest. The Rat smell was very strong, and Billy knew that Rats had been there only a short time before. The fact is, the Rats who owned that nest had discovered Billy Mink and had promptly moved into the house. Billy eagerly followed the trail. It led him to the hole which led in between the walls of the house. Without hesitating a second, Billy popped through, following that scent. It was a queer place. He had never been in such a place before. But Billy knew that where a Rat could go he could go, and so he followed, climbing up between the walls of the house until at last he reached the attic.

He could hear the scampering of many feet and he could hear squeaks of fright, so he knew the Rats knew that he was there. Once in the attic, Billy found the Rat scent everywhere. It was useless to try to follow with his nose, because the Rats had crossed and recrossed each other's paths so often that the trail was all mixed up.

But if Billy couldn't trust to his nose, he could trust to his ears. The sound of scampering feet and the frightened squeaks told him where the Rats were. His eyes blazed with the eager light of the hunter, and without even a glance at all the queer things in that attic, things such as he had never seen before, Billy kept on after those Rats.

Chapter XXXIII

The Farmer Sees a Strange Sight

The really clever folks are those
Who get their friends for them to do
The things they cannot do themselves.
Where'er you go you'll find this true.
Billy Mink.

THE farmer had watched Billy Mink disappear through the hole beneath the shed of the farmhouse. He had chuckled as he saw the tip of Billy's tail disappear. You see, it was to get Billy over to the house that he had made friends with Billy.

For days the farmer had placed food for Billy close to the woodpile under which Billy was living. On this particular morning he had tied a big piece of fish to a string and then had dragged it from the place where he usually left Billy's meals over to the hole under the shed. As you know it hadn't taken Billy long to find that piece of fish.

The farmer hoped that if he could get Billy over to the house, he would follow those Rats and drive them out, just as he had driven them out of the barn. That is why the farmer chuckled when he saw Billy Mink disappear through that hole under the floor of the shed.

It was plain to see that those Rats were
in a terrible fright.   *Page 95.*

For a long time the farmer kept watch, but he was disappointed. Nothing happened. You see, Billy Mink, having eaten a hearty breakfast, had curled up for a nap under the floor of the shed. The farmer didn't know this and so at last he concluded that somehow Billy Mink had slipped out unseen.

"I did hope that little brown rascal would drive those Rats out," muttered the farmer, as he went about his work.

It was some time later in the day that the farmer went to the barn door and glanced over towards the house. Then it was that he saw a strange sight, a very strange sight indeed. Out from that hole through which Billy Mink had entered came a crowd of Rats. There were big Rats, little Rats, and middle-sized Rats. There were gray old grandfather Rats and sleek young Rats. Never had the farmer seen so many Rats at one time.

And it was plain to see that those Rats were in a terrible fright. They were squeaking and squealing with fear, and every one of them was running as fast as he could. They scattered in all directions. Some made for the big barn, some made for the woodpile, some made for the henhouse, and others started off straight toward the next farm, in spite of the snow on the ground. The farmer shouted aloud for joy. He knew there wouldn't be one Rat left in that house by the time Billy Mink came out.

Chapter XXXIV

Billy Goes Home

You'll ne'er regret the kindly deed
That aids another in his need.
Billy Mink.

ALMOST at the heels of the last frightened Rat fleeing from the house of Billy Mink's friend, the farmer, appeared Billy Mink himself. The Rat started for the big barn, but Billy caught him before he was halfway there.

The farmer who had been watching knew that was the last Rat. He knew it because he knew that Billy would not have shown himself outside as long as there was a Rat left inside. At once the farmer went over and stopped up that hole, so that no Rat could get back into the house.

"You killed one of my chickens, you little brown rascal," said he, "but you've paid for it ten times over. I had intended to kill you for that beautiful, brown coat of yours, but now I wouldn't harm a hair of it. As long as you want to stay around here, you are welcome. In fact, the longer you stay around here, the better I will like it, and I shall see to it that you have plenty to eat."

Billy Mink didn't hear this, and he wouldn't have understood it if he had. But he had already made up

his mind that the farmer was his friend and that was
sufficient.

After catching that last Rat to leave the house,
Billy went over to the woodpile where he was making his home. It didn't take him long to discover that
some of those Rats were hiding in the woodpile, and
he promptly hunted them out of there just as he had
hunted them out of the house. Then, being tired, he
curled up for a nap.

For two or three days after that Billy Mink hunted
Rats. He hunted them until there was not one of that
robber gang left in the big barn, the henhouse, or under the woodpile. In fact, there wasn't one of those
robber Rats left on the farm. Where those who had
escaped had gone, the farmer didn't know and Billy
Mink didn't know, and neither of them cared. The
farmer was so happy at being rid of those robbers
that it seemed as if he couldn't do enough for Billy
Mink. He kept Billy supplied with good things to eat,
so that Billy didn't know what it was to be really hungry. He grew as fat as a Mink can be, and he grew lazy
as well.

Now Billy Mink is not naturally lazy. He is one of
the most active of all the little people of the Green
Forest and the Green Meadows. Not having to hunt
for his food, Billy found little to do but eat and sleep,
and after a week of this, he began to get uneasy. He
began to long for excitement and new scenes.

And so one night Billy left his comfortable quar-
ters and started back for the Laughing Brook and

the Smiling Pool, the place he really called home. He was anxious to find out if any of his old friends had been caught in the traps which had been the cause of his leaving the Laughing Brook. The next morning the food put out for him by the farmer was untouched, and the farmer knew that Billy had left, and he was sorry.

Chapter XXXV

Billy Mink Is Quick

Eyes were given us for use;
For failure there is no excuse.
Billy Mink.

WHEN Billy Mink decides to do a thing he wastes no time thinking about it. He does it instantly. Therein he differs from many of his neighbors of the Green Forest. You see, Billy Mink is very quick. He makes quick decisions and he acts just as quickly. That is one reason why Billy is able to go and come as he pleases. There are few he fears.

This doesn't mean that Billy has no enemies who could kill him easily if they caught him. He has several, but he isn't afraid of them simply because he is so quick that he feels sure of being able to escape, even though one of these enemies may surprise him. So it is probable that few, if any, of the little people of the Green Forest and the Green Meadows are filled with fear as seldom as is Billy Mink.

The night he decided to leave the farm where he had been living so well, and go back to the Laughing Brook, he slipped out from under the woodpile almost the instant he had made up his mind. It was a moonlight night, just the kind of a night to travel. Billy bounded along, care-free and happy. As is his way, he stopped to investigate whatever attracted his attention. He looked into every little hole he came to, and when he reached a hollow log he ran through it just to find out if anybody else had used it lately.

By and by, he came to the Green Forest. The moonbeams crept through the branches overhead and there were all sorts of Black Shadows. This was just the kind of a place to suit Billy. Occasionally he ran across a bright open place, but for the most part he kept in the Black Shadows. You see, Billy knows very well that it is difficult for any one to see him in the Black Shadows. Not that he cared particularly who saw him, but he long ago learned that if one is unseen it is much easier to see others.

He was running across one of the bright open places when from the corner of one of his eyes he caught sight of a moving shadow. Now most folks in Billy's place would have stopped, or at least turned to see what that shadow meant. Billy did nothing of the kind. The very second that he caught that glimpse of the moving shadow, Billy bounded off to one side. He didn't hesitate a fraction of a second. Then he darted under a pile of brush, from which he peeped out with his little eyes glowing red with anger. Just over the brush pile Hooty the Owl hovered for an instant, and his great, yellow eyes glared fiercely down into Billy Mink's angry little red ones.

"I almost got you that time," hissed Hooty. "The next time I *will* get you."

"Almost never got anybody yet," snapped Billy. "You'll be an old, old Owl, Hooty, before ever you dine on me." With this, Billy actually darted right out, and before Hooty could turn, was under another pile of brush, laughing at Hooty and making fun of him.

Chapter XXXVI

A Heap of Snow Comes to Life

Appearances sometimes deceive;
Be not too ready to believe.
Billy Mink.

AFTER his adventure with Hooty the Owl, Billy
Mink kept on his way through the Green Forest toward the Laughing Brook. He felt very good. It always makes one feel good to have proven smarter than some one else. Billy had had a very narrow escape. It is doubtful if there was one among Billy's friends who would have escaped had they been in his place. That is because none of them act so quickly as does Billy. It was his quickness which had saved him, for when he had caught sight of that moving shadow, Hooty was already reaching for him with those great, cruel claws of his.

But escapes like this are so common to Billy Mink that he gave no further thought to the adventure. Without any trouble at all, he had given Hooty the Owl the slip, and he knew that Hooty hadn't the least idea in which direction he had vanished. So lightheartedly he continued on his way. But never for an instant did he fail to make use of eyes, ears, and nose to find out what was going on about him.

102

Presently Billy spied off to one side a little white mound under a hemlock tree. It looked very much like other little white mounds scattered here and there. Billy knew that these little mounds were simply snow-covered logs and stumps. They were everywhere through the Green Forest. So Billy paid no particular attention to this little mound and ran past with hardly a glance at it. But he had gone only a few feet when a wandering Little Night Breeze caught up with him and tickled his nose. Instantly Billy Mink turned and with hardly a pause bounded straight toward that little mound. You see, that wandering Little Night Breeze was tickling his nose with a delicious scent. It was the scent of Jumper the Hare.

Billy didn't know where Jumper was, but he knew that all he had to do to find him was to follow that scent with his nose. So Billy bounded along with the eager look of the hunter in his eyes, watching ahead for some sign of Jumper. "I don't see him, but I know he's somewhere near," muttered Billy. "What a blessed thing a good nose is. I don't know what I would do if it were not for mine. Jumper may be ever so well hidden, but my nose will take me straight to him."

He was going straight toward that little mound under the hemlock tree. He was within two jumps of it when suddenly there wasn't any mound there! No, sir, there wasn't any mound there! Instead, a certain little person in white, with long hind legs, was bounding away through the Green Forest. It was Jumper the Hare.

Chapter XXXVII

Jumper the Hare Has a Bad Hour

When once you start a thing to do
Keep at it 'til you see it through.
Billy Mink.

WHEN that little white mound under the hemlock tree suddenly came to life Billy had been surprised. He had known that Jumper the Hare was very near because he had smelled him. But there had been so many little white mounds all about that Billy had paid no special attention to this particular one. As Jumper bounded away Billy Mink chuckled.

"He fooled me that time," muttered Billy. "Jumper certainly fooled me that time. If that wandering Little Night Breeze had not brought the smell of him to me, I would have gone straight on without once suspecting that Jumper was anywhere about. That white coat of his is worth a whole lot to him. I don't doubt he saw me all the time and was laughing to himself as he saw me go past. Well, he laughs best who laughs last. It is a long time since I have had a good run through the Green Forest, and I don't know of any one who can give me a better run than Jumper the Hare."

105

So Billy Mink started after Jumper, his nose to the snow, following the scent Jumper couldn't help leaving. Now Jumper can run much faster than Billy Mink. You know, when he is really frightened, Jumper travels in big leaps. That is how he comes by his name of Jumper. But if Jumper can travel fast, Billy Mink can travel tirelessly, and so right from the start Jumper was worried.

Jumper was worried because he knew that there was not a single place in all the Green Forest where Billy Mink could not follow him. Had it been Old Man Coyote or Reddy Fox in Billy Mink's place, Jumper would not have been nearly so worried. Either of them could run faster than Billy Mink, but there were plenty of places in the Green Forest where neither Old Man Coyote nor Reddy Fox could get at Jumper. You see, there were brush piles under which Jumper could crawl but they could not. But Billy Mink was so small that he could follow wherever Jumper might go, and poor Jumper was worried. His one chance was to make Billy Mink lose his trail.

So Jumper tried all the tricks he knew. He made his jumps just as long as he could, hoping that Billy would lose the scent in between. Round and round through the Green Forest Jumper ran. Every little while he would sit down to rest, but he never had a chance to rest long. In a few minutes a slim brown form would come in sight, running easily and as if not at all tired. Then in a panic Jumper would bound away again.

Now when Jumper ran he ran so fast that he soon grew tired. This was because he was so frightened. Billy Mink, on the other hand, ran easily and did not get at all tired. Billy was enjoying that hunt. It was fun to work out that trail where Jumper tried to mix it up. So, for an hour Billy Mink followed Jumper and had a good time, but it was a bad hour for Jumper.

Chapter XXXVIII

Jumper Is in a Dreadful State of Mind

May fortune spare you from the fate
Of those who find mistakes too late.
Billy Mink.

JUMPER was so intent watching behind him for
Billy Mink that he forgot to keep a sharp watch
ahead of him. The result was that he almost ran into
Old Man Coyote. Old Man Coyote had come over
to the Green Forest, hoping to find Whitefoot the
Wood Mouse or Mrs. Grouse or some one else who
would furnish him with a dinner. So, you can guess
how pleased Old Man Coyote was when he caught
sight of that white form bounding along straight
toward him.

Old Man Coyote crouched as flat as he could right
where he was. He didn't dare move lest Jumper
should see him. "That fellow is in a terrible hurry,"
thought Old Man Coyote. "He acts as if he is scared
half to death. He never runs that way unless some
one is chasing him. I wonder if it can be that Reddy
Fox is hunting over here to-night. Well, it doesn't
make much difference to me who is after Jumper
so long as he drives Jumper right into my mouth. It
looks to me as if I am to have the best dinner of the

whole winter. Goodness knows I need it. It's a long time since I've had a good, square meal."

Straight toward Old Man Coyote, Jumper bounded along. His eyes were rolled back to watch for Billy Mink and he paid no heed at all to what was ahead of him. Now it seemed as if a good fairy must have been watching over Jumper the Hare, for just before he reached Old Man Coyote something prompted him to change his course. He didn't see Old Man Coyote. He didn't know that Old Man Coyote was anywhere about. But something prompted him to change his course, and he turned abruptly to the right.

With a little snarl of disappointment Old Man Coyote sprang after him. The instant he moved, Jumper saw him. Now Old Man Coyote is very swift of foot. Jumper was tired. You know he had been running for an hour. Jumper gave a little shriek of fear and then he headed straight for a brush pile not far off. He reached it none too soon.

With his heart going pit-a-pat, pit-a-pat, pit-a-pat, Jumper crouched under the pile of brush and hope died within him. He had escaped Old Man Coyote, but there was Billy Mink following him. He didn't dare leave the brush pile because of Old Man Coyote, and he didn't dare stay there because of Billy Mink. Jumper was in a dreadful state of mind.

Chapter XXXIX

An Enemy Proves a Friend

Be not too sure lest at the last
Grim disappointment grips you fast.
Billy Mink.

JUMPER the Hare crouched under the big pile of
brush where Old Man Coyote had driven him
and wondered what he should do next. He didn't
dare leave that pile of brush for fear of Old Man
Coyote, and he didn't dare remain there for fear of
Billy Mink. So Jumper was in despair. He couldn't remember ever having been in quite such a bad situa-
tion. Not knowing what to do, he did nothing but sit
still and shake with fright. From where he was he
could peep out. He could see Old Man Coyote sitting down with his head on one side, as if studying
some way to get Jumper out from under that pile of
brush.

For perhaps two minutes Old Man Coyote sat that
way. Suddenly he pricked up his ears and turned
his head. Jumper knew that Old Man Coyote had
heard something. Jumper crept a few steps nearer
the edge of the old pile of brush in order to see out
better. Right away he saw a slim, brown form bounding along toward him. It was Billy Mink.

110

Old Man Coyote was crouched down with his feet set for a quick spring. Jumper knew then that Old Man Coyote had heard Billy Mink coming. It was this that had made him prick up his ears and turn. Billy Mink stopped very abruptly. Then like a flash he turned. He had seen Old Man Coyote, or else he had smelled him. The instant Billy Mink turned, Old Man Coyote sprang forward. There was no place near for Billy Mink to seek safety in save the brush pile where Jumper was and Old Man Coyote was between Billy and that brush pile.

"Old Man Coyote will get him this time," thought Jumper, and didn't know whether to be glad or sorry. He wanted with all his might to be rid of Billy Mink. At the same time he didn't want anything to happen to Billy.

Billy Mink wasted no time looking for a hiding-place. Like a flash he climbed the nearest tree, for you know Billy is a very good climber. There, just out of reach of Old Man Coyote, Billy crouched on a limb and told Old Man Coyote just what he thought of him. Billy was angry clear through. It was one thing to hunt and quite another thing to be hunted. Old Man Coyote didn't seem to mind what Billy Mink said. He sat down at the foot of the tree quite as if he intended to stay there.

Jumper waited to see no more. Very quietly he crept out from under the brush pile on the other side and then took to his heels. He meant to put as great a distance as possible between himself and these two enemies. And as he ran he chuckled. "That's the time an enemy proved a friend," said he, for he knew that he would have nothing more to fear from Billy Mink that night.

Chapter XL

Something Billy Mink Didn't Know

A time there is to run away,
And also there's a time to stay.
Billy Mink.

THE tree up which Billy Mink had scrambled was a big hemlock. He went only high enough to be out of reach of Old Man Coyote, for while Billy can climb easily, he doesn't do any more of this than he has to. He prefers to be on the ground. He will climb readily enough when there is something to climb for, but otherwise he seldom takes the trouble.

Billy was very angry. Old Man Coyote had appeared at just the wrong time. Billy had felt sure that sooner or later he would catch Jumper. But Old Man Coyote had interfered. So Billy spitefully called Old Man Coyote all the bad names he could think of. Old Man Coyote simply looked up at Billy and grinned. "That's a sharp tongue of yours, Billy," said he, "but calling another bad names never yet hurt anybody. I have a mind to keep you up there for a while just to pay you for your impudence."

This is just what Old Man Coyote did. Perhaps he hoped that Billy Mink might lose patience and try to get down. But Billy didn't. He knew when he was well off. He proposed to stay right where he was until Old Man Coyote should lose patience and give up. After a long time Old Man Coyote did give up, and trotted off through the Green Forest.

Then Billy Mink came down. He went at once to the brush pile where Jumper the Hare had hidden, but it didn't take him two minutes to find out that Jumper's trail had grown cold. You see, after a little time the scent left by the foot of an animal disappears. It had been so long since Jumper had left that brush pile that there was no longer any scent where his feet had touched the snow. So Billy Mink gave up in disgust and continued on his way to the Laughing Brook which he soon reached and was once more at home.

Now all the time Billy Mink had been up in the hemlock tree, he had not been alone. He hadn't known this. If he had, he wouldn't have been in such a hurry to come down. Up above his head where the branches were thickest, Mr. and Mrs. Grouse had been roosting. They had been fast asleep when Billy started up the tree, but the sound of his claws on the bark had wakened them instantly. They had been ready to take to their strong wings, if it became necessary, but they were wise enough to keep perfectly still. They liked that big hemlock tree and they felt sure that no one knew that they were in the habit of using it for a roost. So they had sat perfectly still and watched all that happened down below.

When at last Old Man Coyote went away and Billy Mink scrambled down, Mr. and Mrs. Grouse sighed with thankfulness. Then they promptly went to sleep again. Their secret was still their own.

So Billy Mink returned to the Laughing Brook and the Smiling Pool, for you know his heart was really there all the time. I could tell you a great deal more about him and I would like to. But I am not going to, because Little Joe Otter says that he spends more time in the Smiling Pool than Billy Mink does, and that therefore he should have a book in this series. So the next volume will be Little Joe Otter.

THE END

THE END